THE PEASENHALL MURDER

First published 1980
by
Yoxford Publications
Yoxford, Saxmundham, Suffolk.

ISBN 0 907265 01 4

Revised edition 1981
This edition 1992

Designed and set in 11point Trump Medieval by Henry Iles
Printed by Robertson Press, Battersea • London SW11

THE PEASENHALL MURDER

BY EDWIN PACKER

Illustrated by Gary Davis

BIBLIOGRAPHY:

The Trial of William Gardiner, edited by William Henderson, Notable British Trials published by Hodge. Reports in the East Anglian Daily Times and The Eastern Morning Gazette, 1902 and 1903. The Peasenhall Mystery by John Rowland, published by Hutchinson. The Women of Peasenhall, by R.J.White, published by; Macmillan. (Fiction) Genesis 38, by Brian Cooper, published by Heineman. (Fiction)

EDWIN PACKER worked as a journalist in London on various magazines, books and partworks before retiring to Suffolk. He died in January 1980.

The illustrations of Rose Harsent, William Gardiner, the rear of Providence House, the kitchen of Providence House, and of Sibton Chapel have all been copied from sketches that appeared in the East Anglian Daily Times and the Eastern Morning Gazette in 1902 and 1903.

Acknowledgments

No book on the Peasenhall murder could be written without reference to the reports that appeared during 1902 and 1903 in the East Anglian Daily Times published in Ipswich and the Eastern Morning Gazette published in Norwich. I acknowledge the help I have received from reading these reports, and pay tribute to the professional skill of the unnamed journalists who were responsible for them. Another invaluable source has been The Trial of William Gardiner edited by William Henderson and published in the Notable British Trials series.

I would also like to thank Mr B.R.Cole of Framingham Earl, Norwich, for discussing the case with me and for placing his library at my disposal. His knowledge of all the major British criminal trials and of the Peasenhall murder in particular is probably unequalled throughout East Anglia.

E.P.

November 1980

Rose Harsent's gravestone is to be found in the Peasenhall Cemetery which clusters round the old parish church near the centre of the village. The inscription on her stone reads:

In Affectionate
Remembrance of
ROSE ANNIE HARSENT
whose life was cruelly taken
on the 1st of June 1902
in her 23rd year

A light is from our household gone
A voice we loved is stilled,
A place is vacant in our home
That never will be filled.

Stonemasons and newspaper offices keep a list of memorial verses from which the bereaved can select one they think appropriate. The verse chosen by Rose Harsent's family still appears occasionally in the Deaths and In Memoriam columns of East Anglian newspapers.

Rose Harsent.

CHAPTER 1

On the evening of Saturday, May 31st 1902 a thunderstorm moved slowly across East Anglia. At Peasenhall in Suffolk, a village of 700 inhabitants it started shortly after 10 o'clock and did not abate until the early hours of the following morning. Kelly's Directory for 1900 states that Peasenhall is seven miles north-east of Framlingham and the same distance south-west of Halesworth, but today its location is best described by saying that it lies on the A1120, three miles from the junction of that road with the A12 at Yoxford and 27 miles from Stowmarket in the opposite direction.

On that night some of the villagers stood in their doorways watching the gathering storm, gossiping among themselves and with passers-by. One who came to the doorway of his house was 35-year-old William Gardiner, a handsome man with black hair, moustache and beard. He was employed at the Peasenhall Drill Works owned by Smyth & Sons Limited, and by hard work and force of personality had risen from labourer to be foreman of the carpentry department. He was sufficiently well-thought of by his employers to be included in the small party that attended the Paris Exhibition where agricultural machinery made by the firm was on display. Gardiner was also a respected member of the Primitive Methodist connexion. He attended the chapel just over the parish boundary in Sibton, at the end of Poys Street on the opposite side of the road to the White Horse public house. Today the chapel has been taken over by the Peasenhall Youth Club.

Earlier that evening Gardiner had driven John Rickards, the secretary at Smyth & Sons, over to Kelsale in the firm's horse and trap. It was about nine o'clock when he got back and half-past by the time he had stabled the horse at the Drill Works. At home he took off his boots, put on carpet slippers and went to the front door remarking to his wife that a storm was blowing up. He stayed at the front door for some time, and on one occasion walked out into the street where he had a conversation with Harry Burgess, a carpenter, who happened to be passing. They stood talking for about a quarter-of an-hour. Burgess was able to recall this meeting some days later. He said it took place just after 10 o'clock. On leaving Gardiner he walked down the street past The Swan public house, and as he did so he noticed a light in a bedroom window of Providence House.

Providence House (later renamed Stewart House and more recently Stuart House) stands on one corner of the Peasenhall crossroads diagonally opposite Emmetts the grocers. The entrance on the north side faces the main A1120 leading to Badingham, Dennington and Stowmarket; the east side faces Church Street which leads into Rendham Hill. In 1902 the whole length was known as Rendham Hill. It was in the top bedroom on this east side of Providence House that Burgess saw the light burning.

The house seen from Hackney Road is a well-designed building of good proportions, and it comes as a surprise on going round the corner to see that it is semi-detached, built on to the adjoining house and sharing part of a common roof. The house adjoining Providence House was occupied then by a family named Davis. The back yards of the two houses were connected by a gate in the fence.

The occupants of Providence House were Willlam Crisp, a retired tailor, and his wife Georgina. They went to bed that night at 10.15 pm just before the storm started. Mrs Crisp woke up twice during the night. The first time was soon after the storm broke and she got out of bed to see if the rain was coming in at the windows. She went downstairs into the dining room and closed the door between that room and the kitchen. Then she returned upstairs. In the early hours of Sunday morning she awoke a second time on hearing a thud and a scream comingfrom inside the house. The only other person in the house was their servant Rose Harsent, a 23-year-old young woman whose family lived in the village. Rose had a bedroom at the top of the house above the main bedroom occupied by the Crisps.

The village street today.

When she heard the noise Mrs Crisp sat up in bed, roused her husband and prepared to go downstairs. But Mr Crisp dissuaded his wife from investigating. He suggested that the thunder and lightning had frightened Rose, and he reminded his wife that the servant had been told she could always come into their bedroom at any time in the night if she felt nervous.

There was no direct access from the servant's bedroom to that of her master and mistress. Rose's room was reached by a staircase running from the kitchen, and this was the only entrance and exit. In effect the servant was isolated at night from the rest of the household. To get to the bedroom where the Crisps slept, Rose would have to go down this staircase, cross the kitchen and go through a door leading to the main part of the house, and then go up the principal staircase to the Crisps' bedroom.

This explains why Mrs Crisp talked about going downstairs from her bedroom on the first floor to go to the servant's room on the floor above.

At eight o'clock on Sunday morning the following day William Harsent, father of the Crisps' servant, made a routine call on Rose taking clothes that her mother had washed and ironed for her the previous week. As usual Mr Harsent walked up the path to the main door on Hackney Road, turned right there and went round to the back of the house into a small conservatory that was the only means of access to the kitchen from the outside of the house. The door between the conservatory and kitchen was open, and a woollen shawl had been fastened by a fork against the conservatory window. Inside the kitchen Harsent found his daughter lying dead on the floor. Her throat had been cut and there had been an attempt to burn the body.

A few minutes later James Crisp, a shoemaker and brother of Rose Harsent's employer, came to the house and on seeing what had happened raised the alarm. The local police officer, Constable Eli Nunn, arrived at twenty minutes to nine, about the same time as Dr Charles Edward Lay, a surgeon with a practice in Peasenhall.

Rose lay on her back. She was clad in nightdress and stockings and her hair was loosely done up. Her head was close to the stairs that led to her bedroom, and her feet pointed towards the door linking the kitchen with the conservatory. Underneath her head was a copy of the East Anglian Daily Times; part of it was charred, but Rose's hair had not been burnt. Part of her nightdress had also been charred but not the portion that covered her chest and throat. She had three neck wounds. The first extended right across the throat from the angle of the right jaw to the angle of the left jaw. This had completely severed the windpipe. From under the commencement of this wound on the right hand side there was a second wound running upwards underneath the chin. In addition a punctured upward wound had been made from the junction of the angular bone and the breastbone, which joined the big wound across the throat.

On the floor was a considerable amount of blood near the left-hand side of the body. Part of a paraffin lamp on the floor close to the body was moved by William Harsent before he covered his daughter with a rug. The rest of the lamp - the well half-full of oil, the broken glass globe and the broken glass chimney - were a little distance away scattered over the floor. A candlestick holding a burnt-out candle stood some twelve inches from Rose Harsent's head. Broken pieces of a medicine bottle were found about a foot away from the body, and the neck of this bottle with the cork still firmly fixed in it lay about two feet further away, near the kitchen fireplace. Dr Lay picked up the label from the medicine bottle and put it in his pocket for safe keeping.

While awaiting the arrival of his superior officers Constable Nunn went upstairs to search Rose Harsent's bedroom. The bed had not been slept in. Nunn found a number of letters all of which played an important part in subsequent court proceedings. One of these was an unsigned letter of assignation.

> *DR*
>
> *I will try to see you tonight at 12 O'clock at your Place if you Put a light in your window at 10 O'clock for about 10 minutes then you can take it out again. dont have a light in your Room at 12 as I will come round to the back*

There were two letters to the dead young woman signed by William Gardiner, the works foreman and pillar of the Primitive Methodist connexion. They had been written during the month of May the previous year, and were couched in friendly terms though no more than that. They referred to a scandal in the village that had linked the names of Rose Harsent and William Gardiner in the early summer of 1901. Finally there was a bundle of letters containing many references to sexual matters. These were referred to subsequently by members of the legal profession and the police as 'indecent missives' or 'filth'. They were not signed.

The post-mortem examination carried out on Rose by Dr John Charles Ryder Richardson of Saxmundham on June 3rd 1902 showed that she was six-months pregnant at the time of her death.

CHAPTER 2

The gossip linking William Gardiner with Rose Harsent started on the evening of May 1st 1901, a year before her death. On that evening George Wright, aged 20, a wheelwright at the Peasenhall Drill Works, was in Rendham Hill when he saw Rose go along a path leading from the road to a small thatched building that was known generally as the Doctor's Chapel and sometimes as the Green Chapel. This building belonged to the Congregationalists and Rose's employer, William Crisp, was one of its deacons. It was a part of Rose's duties to clean the chapel once a fortnight. It was not her own place of worship. She was a member of the choir of the same Primitive Methodist chapel that Gardiner attended and where he was choirmaster, superintendent of the Sunday School and assistant treasurer of the chapel's trust and school fund.

What follows is Wright's account of the happenings that night, an account to be hotly disputed both by Gardiner and Rose Harsent. Wright's story was that his curiosity was aroused when he noticed William Gardiner turn into the path Rose had taken. He did not stay to find out what might be going on between the two, but hurried off to get an accomplice. If there was anything reprehensible taking place in the Doctor's Chapel it was much more enjoyable for a watcher to have a companion to share that enjoyment.

So Wright ran to get a friend named Alphonso Skinner who was a fitter at the Drill Works. The two of them, young bloods with nothing much to do and possessing - like most of us - a nose for scandal, returned to the Doctor's Chapel. They crept along the path and stood some eight or nine feet from the chapel wall near to one of the ventilators. They professed to have heard two people laughing inside the chapel, then a rustling, and then a woman's voice crying out 'Oh, oh''

At this point Wright went away. He could give no clear reason why he did so. Skinner remained listening; later he maintained he had heard a conversation between the two inside which went something like this:

Woman's voice:	'Did you notice me reading my Bible last Sunday?'
Man's voice:	'What were you reading about?'
Woman's voice:	'I was reading about like what we have been doing tonight. I'll tell you where it is. 38th chapter of Genesis '

Wright said he returned to the chapel after 20 minutes' absence, and that he and Skinner heard a woman say: 'I shall be out tomorrow at nine o'clock, I must go now.' According to them Rose Harsent then came out of the chapel and was followed after an interval by Gardiner.

This was the substance of the story that Wright and Skinner lost no time in spreading through the village. Whether it was true or false, or partly true and much embroidered by them, such a juicy piece of gossip quickly made them the centre of attention. Both Rose and Gardiner subsequently firmly denied the allegations, saying that all Gardiner had done was to close the door of the Chapel at Rose Harsent's request because the door had stuck.

If it had been one of the lads of the village who followed Rose to the Chapel not much attention would have been paid to the story. But Gardiner's status in Peasenhall - a married man with six children, a foreman at the local works, above all a leading member of the Primitive Methodist chapel - gave piquancy to the account put out by Wright and Skinner.

The Doctors' Chapel.

When the gossip finally got back to Gardiner he asked the two young men to come to his office at the works. 'What's this you have set afloat about me?' he said. They repeated the story they had been spreading. Gardiner denied that any such thing had happened, and he demanded an apology from both of them. But Wright and Skinner declined to apologise and refused to withdraw anything they had said.

Gardiner then wrote to Rose:

Dear Rose,
I was very much surprised this morning to hear that there's some scandal going the round about you and me going into the Doctor's Chapel for immoral Purposes so that I shall put it into other hands at once as I have found out who it was that started it. Bill Wright and Skinner say they saw us there but I shall summons them for defamation of character unless they withdraw what they have said and give me a written apology. I shall see Bob tonight and we will come and see you together if possible. I shall at the same time see your father and tell him.

Yours &c., William Gardiner.

Primitive Methodists in the area were disconcerted by what was going on, believing that it reflected on the good name of chapel folk. They decided to hold an enquiry into the affair.
It took place at Sibton Chapel on May 11th 1901, with John Guy, the superintendent minister of

the Wangford Circuit presiding. Wright and Skinner consented to attend although they were not Methodists, but Rose Harsent did not go. We do not know the reason for this; possibly it was because she could not get away from her domestic duties at Providence House, or she may not have wished to appear before the tribunal. She was, however, interviewed by John Guy some days later and she denied the story.

The enquiry resulted in deadlock. The two young men repeated their allegations and were questioned by members of the committee of enquiry. Gardiner strongly refuted the accusations. It was the word of two accusers against that of the two accused.

Feeling it was the right thing to do, Gardiner resigned all the offices he held at the Chapel, but he was re-elected at a quarterly meeting held about a month later. This demonstrated that chapel members believed him to be telling the truth, or at least thought that the accusations against him remained unproven.

On the day of the chapel enquiry into the affair Gardiner wrote again to Rose:

Dear Rose,
I have broke the news to Mrs Gardiner this morning, she is awfully upset but she say she know it is wrong, for I was at home from 1/2 past 9 o'clock so I could not possibly be with you an hour so she wont believe anything about it. I have asked Mr Burgess to ask those too Chaps to come to Chapel tonight and have it

out there however they stand by such a tale I dont know but I dont think God will forsake me now and if we put our trust in Him it will end right but its awfully hard work to have to face people when they are all suspicious of you but by God's help whether they believe me or not I shall try and live it down and prove by my future conduct that its all false, I only wish I could take it to Court but I dont see a shadow of a chance to get the case as I dont think you would be strong enough to face a trial. Trusting that God will direct us and make the way clear

- I remain, yours in trouble, W Gardiner.

These were the two letters signed by Gardiner that Constable Nunn found in Rose's bedroom. Although in his second letter Gardiner had indicated that he would not take legal proceedings against Wright and Skinner, he did go through the preliminary motions. He consulted Harold A. Mullen, a solicitor in Halesworth, and Mullen wrote to the two youths threatening them with legal process unless they gave a written apology. Wright and Skinner were not intimidated by this. They did not apologise and no legal proceedings were taken against them. The reasons given later by Gardiner for not going to court was that this would incur considerable expense, and he knew that if his accusers were convicted of slander they had no means to pay his costs, let alone any damages that might have been awarded.

CHAPTER 3

It is easy to be critical of an official investigation that took place 80 years ago. Nevertheless, given the circumstances surrounding Rose Harsent's death it seems incredible that the police should have thought at first that the young woman killed herself. We do not know what made them favour the suicide theory. Were they influenced, perhaps, by Dr Lay? At the inquest Dr Lay would not commit himself when asked if the wounds on Rose's neck could have been self-inflicted, but he did say that the fleshy part of the neck wound could have been made by glass. At the adjourned hearing a fortnight later he had come to the conclusion that the wounds were not self-inflicted and that glass was *not* responsible for the injuries.

Two of the letters in the bedroom connected Gardiner with Rose, so one would have thought that immediate contact would have been made with him. Even if the letters had not been found Gardiner should have been interviewed

The conservatory at the back of Providence House.

without delay, because Constable Nunn who was stationed at Peasenhall was fully aware - as was everybody else in the village–that gossip had linked the names of Gardiner and the dead young woman a year ago. The constable knew too that there had been an enquiry by the officials of the Sibton Chapel into the alleged association of the two.

In spite of this the suicide theory was allowed at the outset to influence both the handling of the investigation and the pace at which it was carried out.

Gardiner was not spoken to by the police until the following day, Monday, June 2nd, and then not at his home but at his place of employment. If Rose Harsent had been murdered and if Gardiner was the man responsible then he had been allowed more than 24 hours to conceal or destroy incriminating evidence. He was not arrested until Tuesday evening, by which time - had he been guilty - he would have had three days to cover his tracks.

Constable Nunn paid the first police visit to the Gardiner home shortly after 10 o'clock on Monday morning, June 2nd, to question Mrs. Gardiner about her husband's movements on the preceding Saturday night. He returned again three hours later, this time accompanied by two of his superiors, Superintendent George Sidney Staunton and Inspector Berry. The object of this visit was the same - to ask Mrs Gardiner where her husband was between the time he left work on Saturday until eight o'clock on Sunday morning. Superintendent Staunton was to admit later that no notes were taken at this interview because the suicide theory was still strongly held. The police did not search Gardiner's house, nor at that time were any of his clothes taken away for examination.

At four o'clock that afternoon the police paid a third visit to the Gardiner home. Inspector Staunton had just heard about the label on the medicine bottle that Dr Lay had put in his pocket for safe keeping when the body was found. Staunton asked Mrs Gardiner for a medicine bottle having on the label 'Mrs Gardiner's sister'. Mrs Gardiner could not find it, but she told the police: 'I offered to give Rose Harsent some camphorated oil, and I may have put it in that bottle; I am not sure whether she took it away.'

Although during these interviews Gardiner had been kept under unofficial detention at the Drill Works, he was allowed to return home in the evening at the usual time. He was arrested at half-past eight the following night. On this occasion the police thought fit to take some of Gardiner's clothes - a coat, undervest, dirty shirt and trousers. In the trousers the accused man was wearing was found a two-bladed pocket knife, and this was sent to the senior official analyst at the Home Office, Dr Thomas Stevenson, for examination.When the warrant for his arrest was read over to Gardiner he replied: 'I am not guilty'.

CHAPTER 4

C.W.Chaston, the coroner for the area, opened the inquest on Rose Harsent at The Swan public house, Peasenhall, on Tuesday June 3rd, the same day that Gardiner was arrested. The man who signed the warrant was the local landowner, squire and magistrate Captain E.B.Levett Scrivener, and he too was the foreman of the Coroner's jury. This did not seem to arouse comment at the time, but when the inquest was resumed later in the month Captain Levett Scrivener asked if he could be excused from jury duty. The Coroner refused.

At the inquest some facts about Rose Harsent

did emerge. Her parents gave evidence, and from what they said it appears she was engaged to be married in 1900. They had questioned Rose some weeks before her death, suspecting she was pregnant. She denied it.

Police enquiries were still taking place so it was not possible for the Coroner's court to reach a verdict on the incomplete evidence placed before it. They adjourned proceedings to June 16th; once again there was an obstacle to reaching a verdict. The Director of Public Prosecutions had informed the Coroner that if certain evidence was given at the resumed inquest it would influence the committal proceedings at the Magistrates Court fixed for June 20th. One minor point of interest emerged from the resumed inquest. A police officer stated that the distance from Providence House to Gardiner's home was 208 yards and that it could be walked in 4 minutes 12 seconds. The inference was that if Gardiner had slipped out of his own house on the night of the murder he could have committed the crime and returned home again in less than 10 minutes. But such timing did not allow for any hitch or delay in the murder operation.

Gardiner appeared before the Magistrates Court at Saxmundham on June 20th. On the bench were J.K.Brooke of Sibton Park (chairman) Lieut. Colonel H. Abdy Collins of Saxmundham and H.M.Doughty of Theberton. The court had to decide whether the evidence was strong enough to warrant sending Gardiner for trial at the Assizes. Both prosecution and defence were in the hands of Ipswich solicitors, E.P.Ridley appearing for the Crown and A.S. Leighton for the defence. At the outset a provocative statement was made by Mr Ridley who stated that for the past year the prisoner and Rose Harsent had been having 'immoral relations'. Mr Leighton for the defence strongly objected to this, saying that such statements

The Swan public house where the inquest was held.

should not be made unless they were going to be proved. Mr Ridley contended that the witnesses he would call would prove it - but the evidence did nothing of the kind, merely being a repeat of the Wright and Skinner allegations. Of definite proof there was none.

Mr Leighton, hoping to get the case against his client dismissed at this court, continued throughout the hearing to attack the prosecution's statements. As all the evidence for the Crown was circumstantial the defence endeavoured to raise doubts in the minds of the listeners on every issue. But no decision was reached that day. The hearing was adjourned until July 3rd.

So the official game of leap-frog went on, with an unconvicted prisoner still in custody. The inquest had been adjourned to allow for the magistrates' hearing, and now the magistrates adjourned for the Coroner to complete the inquest on June 30th. The main reason for the delay was that the police had not sufficient grounds to secure a conviction; they were still making enquiries among the residents of Peasenhall and district to strengthen the chain of circumstantial evidence against the prisoner.

The inquest held at The Swan public house had been an uncomfortable experience for everyone, for the accommodation was quite inadequate. The adjourned hearing took place at the Peasenhall Assembly Rooms on Hackney Road, facing the junction of the Bruisyard Road with the A1120. Some new faces were seen in the witness box. Mrs Rosanna Dickenson, Gardiner's next-door neighbour, said she saw Rose Harsent go to the back door of the Gardiner house at 9 pm on the night of the thunderstorm. But she did not go inside as neither Mr or Mrs Gardiner were at home - Gardiner had driven over to Kelsale and his wife had gone to the village shop that she always kept open late on Saturday nights.

James Morriss, an assistant gamekeeper in the employ of Captain Levett Scrivener, testified that in the early hours of Sunday he had seen two sets of footprints leading to and from Gardiner's house to Providence House, and that they had been made by rubber-soled shoes with bars across the treads. Wouldn't any footprints on a hard macadamed road have been washed out by the heavy rain? asked the defence solicitor. Morriss stuck to his story. They weren't washed out because he saw them.

The defence solicitor hoped the Coroner's jury would return a verdict that did not name Gardiner, such as murder by a person or persons unknown. This was not to be. The jury brought in a unanimous verdict of murder, naming William Gardiner. So back to the final sitting of the Magistrates Court at Saxmundham on July 3rd, 1902. This time there were four magistrates on the bench, D. Parry Crooke of Darsham and Captain George Edward Price, R.N. of Carlton, joining two who had been at the earlier hearing, J.K. Brooke and Lieut-Colonel Abdy Collins.

The most significant piece of evidence not heard before was that given by Dr Stevenson, the Home Office analyst. The clothes belonging to Gardiner that had been sent to Dr Stevenson were completely free of blood and paraffin. A very small piece of bloodstained cloth, three-sixteenths of an inch across, which had been attached to a broken piece of glass was a different sort of cloth from that of Gardiner's clothes, and there was I10 hole in the prisoner's jacket and trousers from which this cloth could have come. Dr Stevenson added that there were traces of mammalian blood on Gardiner's pocket knife, but he could not say how old it was or whether for certain it was human blood. Here again was an element of doubt.

The magistrates committed Gardiner for trial at the next Assizes at County Hall, Ipswich on November 7th 1902. Two of the magistrates, Crooke and Price, had heard only half of the evidence, not having been present at the hearing on June 20th.

According to a reporter from the East Anglian Daily Times the prisoner and his wife were allowed a few minutes together in an ante-room before Gardiner returned to prison. Both were in tears.

CHAPTER 5

The first trial of William Gardiner took place at Ipswich between November 7th and 10th, 1902. Counsel for the prosecution was H.F.Dickens, a son of Charles Dickens the novelist. During the trial he stayed at the Great White Horse in Ipswich, the hotel mentioned by Charles Dickens in Pickwick Papers. A K.C. since 1892, he was more experienced than the defence counsel Ernest E. Wild, who had only recently been called to the Bar. The judge was a former Conservative Member of Parliament, Sir William Grantham.

Two witnesses were called by the prosecution

who had not been found in time for the Magistrates Court, so it was clear the police were having difficulty in building up a satisfactory case against Gardiner. The two were Henry Rouse, a Sibton labourer and like Gardiner - a pillar of the Primitive Methodist connexion, and Herbert Stammers whose house lay up an alley alongside the Gardiner home.

At one point the jury asked to see the letters Gardiner had written to his wife from prison, so that they could judge if the handwriting resembled that of the assignation letter found in Rose's bedroom. The letters were at Gardiner's home in Peasenhall. So the court despatched A.F. Garnham, a garage proprietor of Woodbridge Road, Ipswich, to fetch them. He was given to understand that he would not be prosecuted for exceeding the speed limit. He covered the 43-mile journey by car in three hours, the return journey taking just under one hour.

According to William Henderson, editor of ***The Trial of William Gardiner*** in the Notable British Trials series published by Hodge, the summing-up of the judge at this first trial was against the accused and strongly in favour of conviction. Nevertheless the jury could not agree. One juryman was against convicting Gardiner, and he made his position clear in the courtroom by stating: 'I have heard nothing to convince me that the prisoner is guilty.' Gardiner was again remanded in custody to await a fresh trial in the New Year.

What strikes the modern reader about one

William Gardiner.

section of Henderson's introduction to ***The Trial of William Gardiner*** are the generalisations he makes based on no evidence whatsoever. He maligns East Anglian folk by writing 'living as she (Rose Harsent) did in a part of England not notably celebrated for a particularly high standard of moral purity.' By 'moral' he means 'sexual' and he produces no proof for such a sweeping statement. He calls Rose 'an attractive girl of East Anglian type' although it has never been demonstrated that there is such a thing as an East Anglian type of beauty.

Chapter 6

We do not know who helped Mrs Gardiner to find the money to pay for her husband's defence at the first trial. At the end of that time she was penniless, and she and her children were receiving relief from the Parish. How was she to obtain money for the defence at the second trial? Someone - probably Gardiner's solicitor - suggested that she should write a letter to the Times appealing for funds.

On November 15th 1902 this letter appeared:

I am the wife of William Gardiner, accused of the Peasenhall murder. I have six children. My husband has been in prison for more than five months, and during that time my children and I have received parish relief. What little money I could get together went to pay for my husband's defence, and now I am penniless and heartbroken. I know that my husband is innocent, and I cannot allow him to go undefended, if it can be avoided, at his next trial. Would you help me, and ask the public also to help me? P. S. The editor of the East Anglian Daily Times, Ipswich, has been so good as to promise to acknowledge contributions.

The East Anglian Daily Times gave whole-hearted support to the appeal, and did even more than ***The Times*** - it acknowledged every contribution in its columns. Several hundreds of pounds poured in.

This money enabled Gardiner to be represented at his second trial once again by Ernest E. Wild and H. Claughton Scott, they having been instructed on Gardiner's behalf by Leighton and Aldous, solicitors, of Arcade Street, Ipswich. The case for the Crown was once again in the hands of H.F.Dickens, K.C., and John de Grey. Proceedings got under way at Ipswich on

Wednesday, January 21st 1903, before Mr Justice Lawrance, or the Honourable John Compton Lawrance to give him his full title, formerly a Conservative Member of Parliament representing one of the Lincolnshire divisions.

Mr Dickens opened by saying that the Crown had to satisfy the jury of the guilt of the prisoner 'and if there is any reasonable doubt arising from the evidence then the Crown have not fulfilled their duty and have not satisfied the burden which is upon the Crown to prove this man's guilt.' The task of the defence was to cast doubt upon that evidence.

The Peasenhall murder had aroused interest throughout the country and reporters from many national newspapers were present. However, the fullest accounts, verbatim reports of the trial (and the one that had preceded it) came from journalists on the ***East Anglian Daily Times*** and the ***Eastern Morning Gazette***. Reading their account and pen pictures of personalities at the Assizes it is possible to get a better impression of the proceedings than can be gained from the official account to be found in the ***Notable Trial Series***. This is how the ***East Anglian Daily Times*** reporter described William Gardiner: 'He is a man of striking and rather intelligent appearance. His forehead is very broad and moderately high; his eyes are black and piercing; nose large and slightly aquiline; the hair and complexion so intensely dark as to suggest the Spaniard rather than the Englishman.'

The first major witness for the prosecution, in

what the Crown hoped would be a chain of evidence against Gardiner, was George Wright, one of the two young men who had spread the gossip about the prisoner in May 1901. Wright did not find it much of an ordeal. He had told his story at the Chapel enquiry, at the Magistrates Court and at the first trial, and now he was being led through the same recital. There is no need to repeat it here as it has been given earlier on in this book. The witness's self-assurance was amply demonstrated when he was being cross-examined by Mr Wild, who wanted to know what motive Wright and Skinner had in listening outside the Doctor's Chapel. 'Did you go along expecting to hear something indecent?' asked defence counsel. 'We did not expect to hear a sermon.' Wright replied perkily.

It appeared that Wright knew Rose Harsent quite well. He had been to Providence House doing odd jobs, and had spoken to her there, but he swore he had never walked out with her. Mr Wild also obtained from Wright an admission that some years before he had spread gossip about a young man and a girl whom he had seen go into an orchard together. Alphonso Skinner who followed Wright into the witness box confirmed his friend's evidence, and then related the conversation only he had heard about the 38th chapter of Genesis.

Already defence counsel had managed to introduce an element of doubt in the minds of the listeners. Wright had testified that Gardiner saw him quite plainly before he turned into the path to the Doctor's Chapel. If Gardiner was having a clandestine affair with Rose Harsent is it likely he would join her in the Chapel and have sexual intercourse with her if he had been seen by Wright, knowing such an action would arouse suspicion? Secrecy is essential in such matters.

The evidence of John Guy, superintendent minister of the Methodist circuit, then followed. Guy had presided over the enquiry into Wright and Skinner's allegations in May 1901, and the outcome of this enquiry appeared to be in Gardiner's favour. The Crown knew this. Its purpose in calling Guy for the prosecution was to demonstrate that the enquiry did not absolve Gardiner; it had only said that no definite conclusion could be reached. The prosecution apparently succeeded in showing that this was so, and was also able to get the witness to testify about a private conversation he had had with Gardiner after the enquiry. The prisoner admitted then that he had accompanied Rose Harsent home from chapel on several occasions, that he (Gardiner) had been indiscreet, and that in future he would be more careful.

Yet when Mr Wild had finished his cross-examination a different light had been thrown on this evidence. John Guy agreed that the full extent of Gardiner's 'indiscretion' was the admission that choirmaster and choir member had walked home after chapel meetings, and that he (Guy) saw nothing wrong in this, for their homes lay in the same direction. All that Gardiner's promise to be more discreet amounted to was that he would not walk home with Rose Harsent again. So the jury was being invited to doubt the prosecution's case that Gardiner had made damaging admission. It was nothing of the kind, merely that he had been made aware that some people in the village would deliberately misconstrue innocent conduct, and that he must be on his guard.

Another Methodist preacher, Henry Rouse, a 73-year old labourer living at Sibton, was next in the box. This witness had not given evidence before the magistrates. He stated that about a quarter-to-nine one night in February 1902 he had met Gardiner and Rose Harsent when he was on his way home from Yoxford. Rouse stated he bade them 'goodnight' but that neither had replied, and that furthermore when he spoke to Gardiner about it some nine days later the prisoner had promised it would never occur again if Rouse would say nothing about it.

This was important evidence, if true, but Rouse then cast doubt on his character as a believable witness by recounting another incident. He alleged that at a Sunday evening service at the Sibton Chapel,when he was preaching, he had seen Gardiner put his feet into Rose Harsent's lap during the sermon. He did not stop speaking in order to reprimand Gardiner, neither did he mention the matter to the two concerned afterwards. Instead he got his wife to write an anonymous letter to Gardiner warning him about his behaviour - but making no reference to the feet-in-lap incident.

Providence House. (Rose's room top right)

Mr Wild had no difficulty in showing this witness to be an extremely eccentric character, and in creating doubt as to his veracity Rouse at the first trial had made no mention of Gardiner promising to give up seeing Rose Harsent. So had Rouse invented this while waiting for the second trial? Defense counsel was also able to get from Rouse an admission that eight or nine members of the choir could have seen Gardiner rest his feet in Rose Harsent's lap. Finally Rouse was questioned about three incidents in his past life which showed him to be a mischief maker. It is doubtful if Rouse did the case for the Crown any good.

Harry Harsent, the 14-year-old brother of the dead woman, was called to prove that Gardiner had been corresponding with Rose. He had carried letters from the prisoner to her. In 1901 he had taken two or three letters, and one or two from his sister to Gardiner, and in 1902 he had taken two letters from Gardiner to Rose. Yet under cross-examination he admitted that at the first trial he had sworn he had not taken any letters during 1902. In the interval between the two trials had someone been trying to help young Harsent improve his memory?

Mrs Georgina Crisp of Providence House was called by the prosecution presumably to help establish the time of Rose Harsent's death. If it could be shown that Gardiner had been absent from his home about the time when Mrs Crisp heard the thud and scream in the early hours of Sunday, then the prosecution had forged a strong link in its chain of circumstantial evidence. Yet Mr Dickens did not question her regarding the time; perhaps he had had second thoughts on the matter. It was left to the defence counsel to show that the witness did not know what time it was during the night when she heard the thud and scream. She admitted that at the Coroner's inquest she had said it was between twelve and one when she first went downstairs to close the windows against the rain. Now she admitted she had been guided by her husband in this; she had not looked at the clock herself. She admitted, too, that at the Magistrates Court she had testified that she could not say at what time she heard the thud and scream, although at the inquest she had stated it was between one and two o'clock *on* the Sunday morning, because her husband thought it was about that time.

The obvious person to call would have been Mr Crisp, but the Crown did not do this. No reason was given. Mr Crisp was deaf, but deafness is not a bar to giving testimony. Indeed, Mr Crisp was in court when his wife was being badgered by Mr Wild, and he heard quite well what was being said. At one point he stood up and asked if he could speak and was peremptorily told to sit down and be quiet. So the defence succeeded in instilling doubt in the minds of the jury. If the time of the dead woman's murder was not known it would be the more difficult to prove that Gardiner was at Providence House at the crucial time - for nobody knew what the crucial time was.

If the Crown had hoped that expert medical witnesses would pinpoint the time of the death that hope was not realised. Dr Lay, who had first seen the body at about a quarter-to-nine on the Sunday morning, said that death had taken place at least four hours before, but agreed under cross-examination that there had been instances when rigor mortis had been delayed by as much as twelve hours. He found it impossible to say whether Rose Harsent had been dead four or eight hours when he first saw the body. Dr Stevenson, the Home Office analyst, thought that in the British climate rigor mortis would set in after about five hours, but in the summer it might be between eight and twelve hours.

Dr Stevenson also gave evidence about the mammalian blood found on Gardiner's pocket knife. He examined the knife on June 9th and he formed the opinion the blood had been on it not more than a month, but he declined to stake his professional reputation on this opinion when invited to do so under cross-examination. He stated, too, that mammalian blood need not necessarily mean human blood - for example, it could be that of a rat.

Harry Burgess, a Peasenhall bricklayer, the man who had had a chat with Gardiner shortly after 10 o'clock on Saturday, May 31st when the prisoner was standing outside his front door, testified to this effect. He was the only witness who had seen the light in Rose Harsent's bedroom window that night. The inference that the prosecution hoped the jury would draw from this evidence was that Gardiner too could have seen the light in the window. If he had written the letter of assignation then it was to be expected he would be in the main street looking for the signal from Rose Harsent's bedroom.

Burgess had taken part, later, in an experiment organised presumably by the police when he, Constable Nunn, Wright and Skinner, had gone to the Doctor's Chapel to verify that anyone speaking inside the Chapel could be heard outside. The experiment took place on July 18th, some eight weeks after the murder. That such a length of time should have been allowed to elapse reflects the leisurely pace at which the police proceeded to gather evidence. To check Wright and Skinner's story immediately after the murder would have seemed the obvious course, for if the two young men were lying any association between the prisoner and the dead woman would be in question. But Burgess's evidence was of little value either to prosecution or defence. He had gone inside the Chapel and had listened to Wright and Skinner talking there. He had not stood outside trying to hear what they were saying.

Constable Eli Nunn had been in charge of that particular experiment. He stationed himself outside the Doctor's Chapel in the place where Wright and Skinner indicated they stood, while the two men went inside and pretended to be Gardiner and Rose Harsent. Not unexpectedly they succeeded in making Constable Nunn hear what they said.

Later in the trial this evidence was called into question by defence witnesses who had conducted a similar but much more thorough experiment. Arthur Sadleir Leighton, Gardiner's solicitor, went to the Doctor's Chapel with two friends. They took it in turns to stand where Wright and Skinner said they stood, while the other two went inside the Chapel and read alternate verses from the hymn book in a speaking voice. Mr Leighton testified that all he could hear when outside the Chapel was a murmur; he could not distinguish a single word. Later Mr Leighton went again to the Chapel and repeated the experiment with two other men. The same course was adopted and the same result obtained. No conversation could be distinguished if the speakers inside the Chapel spoke in an ordinary tone of voice. Once again doubt had been cast on the prosecution's evidence.

Mr Leighton also testified that on the occasion of his first visit to the Doctor's Chapel he noticed there were signs of the door of the Chapel having been planed. He had called attention to this fact to William Crisp, a deacon at the Doctor's Chapel and Rose Harsent's employer. This was in June 1902, and the Chapel incident had taken place a year before.

We must now return to the remainder of Constable Nunn's evidence. After describing the scene in the kitchen of Providence House when he arrived there on the morning of the murder, and of his discovery of numerous letters in the bedroom, he recounted the visits he had paid to Gardiner's house in the early days of the enquiry. He went there twice before Gardiner was arrested. On the first occasion, early on the Monday morning, Mrs Gardiner gave him an account of her husband's movements on the night of the thunderstorm. The second time was about one o'clock on the Monday when Nunn was accompanied by Superintendent Staunton and Inspector Berry. Once again they went over the events of the Saturday night with Mrs Gardiner. There had been little or no discrepancy between the story told by Gardiner when questioned at his place of work and the account given by his wife. On the following day the police paid a third visit to Mrs Gardiner to question her about the medicine bottle found near Rose Harsent's body. Mrs Gardiner told the police she was a great believer in camphorated oil as a remedy for colds, and at Easter 1902, when Rose had a bad cold she (Mrs Gardiner) had given Rose a medicine bottle with some camphorated oil in it. Nunn stated that the broken medicine bottle found near Rose Harsent's body carried a label that Dr Lay had put in his pocket for safe keeping. The Clerk of the Court then read out the inscription on the label which Dr Lay had later handed to Superintendent Staunton. It ran: *'Two or three teaspoonfuls, a sixth part, to be taken every four hours - Mrs Gardiner's children.'*

Nunn had arrested Gardiner at half-past eight on the evening of Tuesday, June 3rd, two-and-a-half days after the body of Rose had been discovered. On that occasion - Nunn's fourth visit to the house - he had taken away a coat, undervest, dirty shirt and a pair of trousers belonging to the prisoner, and a white- handled two-bladed pocket knife. On the following day he had taken away a pair of boots and a pair of carpet slippers. Having then heard, by way of a brother of Redgrave, the head gamekeeper, of James Morriss's story of footprints made by india-rubber shoes, Nunn went yet again and was given a pair of india-rubber shoes together with an old black coat and vest by Mrs Gardiner. She told the police officer that her brother had given them these shoes but that her husband had never worn them. Constable Nunn agreed that

Mrs Gardiner had always given him whatever articles of clothing he had asked for.

Mrs Gardiner's statement to Nunn concerning her husband's movements on the night of the storm was as follows:

> *'My husband left home about half-past two returned home at 9.30, had his supper, went with me to Mr and Mrs Dickenson's and stayed there until 1.30, went to bed, and did not leave home until 8.30 next morning'.*

There was a slight discrepancy in the statement on the same subject she made later to Superintendent Staunton. She told Staunton, referring to the visit to the Dickensons next door: 'I went in first, and he came shortly afterwards.' To get to the Dickinsons' house the Gardiners had to cross an alley between the two dwellings. They usually went from their back door to the side door of the neighbouring house.

Mrs Rosanna Dickenson said that Mrs Gardiner had gone to her house at between 11 and 11.30 pm and that Gardiner had followed between 11.45 and midnight. Gardiner, giving evidence later, thought the time that elapsed before he followed his wife next door was much less than this; he had stayed behind to go upstairs to look at the children, making sure they were asleep. Mrs Gardiner in her evidence agreed with her husband; although she did not look at the time she judged that her husband followed her to the Dickensons a few minutes

William Gardiner's house.

afterwards. The prosecution was trying to establish that Gardiner, having fixed the appointment with Rose for midnight, had managed to get to Providence House, murder her, and return home very soon afterwards. But the testimony of Mrs Dickenson and Mrs Gardiner did not support this supposition; according to them Gardiner had certainly been in the Dickenson home at midnight - the time he had allegedly arranged to be with Rose Harsent.

The defence was able to show, too, that Gardiner could not have gone to Providence House in the early hours of Sunday morning. On returning from the Dickensons the Gardiners went upstairs and undressed. Mrs Gardiner gave evidence that she had heard the church clock strike two at the time they were getting into bed. Then their young son Bertie woke up, and his mother went into his bedroom to quieten him. Soon afterwards she got out of bed again because she had a severe pain, and she went downstairs to get some brandy. On getting into bed the third time she looked at the bedroom clock and remarked to her husband that it was twenty-past two. Although Gardiner went to sleep she was not able to do so on account of the pain, and she remained awake until she heard the church clock strike five. So if Mrs Gardiner's evidence was to be believed her husband could not possibly have left the bedroom that night.

Some corroboration came from a defence witness, Mrs Amelia Pepper, next-door neighbour of the Gardiners on the other side. Their houses adjoined, and the main bedrooms of the two were separated by only a thin partition. Mrs Pepper testified that on the night of the thunderstorm she had heard the Gardiners go to bed just before two o'clock. Later she heard Bertie Gardiner scream and then Mrs Gardiner could be heard speaking to him. She heard Mrs Gardiner go downstairs. Being a very nervous woman and frightened by the storm, she got up at twenty-past two and went downstairs into the front room of the house where she stayed until a quarter-past four. During that time she did not hear any door open or shut, nor did anyone pass her front door.

The prosecution tried to shake this evidence by reminding Mrs Pepper of a statement to Superintendent Staunton to the effect that she had

had a conversation with Mrs Gardiner on the Sunday morning, and that was how she knew it was Mrs Gardiner who had gone downstairs. But now in the witness box Mrs Pepper implied that the police superintendent had misconstrued her remarks; she had definitely heard Mrs Gardiner go downstairs. Having been a next-door neighbour for three years, living in a house with a very thin dividing wall, she was able from experience to tell the footsteps of the next-door neighbours, and could distinguish quite well between those of Mr and Mrs Gardiner.

During the examination of Mrs Dickenson and Mrs Pepper by Mr Dickens the prosecution shifted its ground and presented the jury with a choice of times for the committal of the murder. At first the suggestion underlying the questions put to Mrs Dickenson was that Gardiner went to Providence House just before midnight at a time when he was supposed to be seeing if his children were asleep. Later, when Mrs Pepper was in the witness box, the drift of the prosecution's cross-examination was that it was Gardiner whom Mrs Pepper had heard going downstairs shortly after two o'clock, and it was then he had gone out of the house to visit Rose. This hint of uncertainty on the part of the Crown could not have helped its case.

James Morriss, the assistant gamekeeper at Peasenhall, who had testified at the Magistrates Court about his discovery of footprints from Providence House to Gardiner's house, repeated the evidence he had given earlier. If members of the jury believed the testimony of the Gardiners and their two next door neighbours that Gardiner had not left his home on the night of the murder, what were they to make of the story Morriss had to tell? The footprints made by india-rubber shoes had started, according to him, just outside Gardiner's house - though not on the wide doorstep - had continued to the front of Providence House, and another set of prints ran in opposite direction. He had noticed both sets of prints at the same time while he was walking along Peasenhall Street past Gardiner's house towards Hackney Road.

He had reported this to Mr Redgrave, the head gamekeeper, at a quarter-to-six in the morning of Sunday, June 1st, shortly after he said he had seen them, and several hours before the news of Rose Harsent's murder became known. He could not explain why, in possession of what appeared to be most important evidence, he did not go to the police when he heard of the murder at Providence House. He agreed that if the police had not come to him having heard the story from a third party - he would very likely have not mentioned it to them.

As we know Constable Nunn did collect a pair of india-rubber shoes from Mrs Gardiner after her husband had been arrested. The prosecution would have the jury believe that these were the shoes that made the footprints allegedly seen by Morriss, but there was no way of knowing if they fitted the prints Morriss said he had seen.

Another witness who had seemingly important evidence and who, like Morriss, had made no effort to inform the police of it, was Herbert Stammers. The alley that divided the Gardiner and Dickinson houses led to the house occupied by this witness. From the front of his house he could look on to the back yard of the Gardiners. When the police interviewed him, having heard his story from a third party, he told them that he had seen a large fire in the wash-house in the Gardiners' back yard with smoke coming out of the chimney, on Sunday morning, the 1st of June at about 7.30. He had seen fires there on other Sunday mornings but never so early - usually at eight or half-past. The prosecution was making the point that the prisoner was burning something - clothing perhaps.

Both the prisoner and his wife were questioned about this evidence later when the defence presented its case. It was their custom, they said, to light the wash-house fire on Sunday mornings in the summer in order to boil water for the morning tea. They did not use the kitchen fire as they liked to keep the house cool. On the Sunday in question Gardiner had lit the fire - only a small wood fire, no coal, shortly after eight o'clock, certainly not before. Gardiner was emphatic that the story told by Stammers was a deliberate lie. He added that he and Stammers had been neighbours for three or four years: 'We never had any connexions with one another. I knew him just to give him "the seal of the day" but no further.'

Why Frederick James Davis should have been called by the Crown as a witness is difficult to understand. He had nothing to contribute to the case against Gardiner. The police had discovered he was the writer of the 'indecent missives' - the unsigned bundle of letters found in Rose Harsent's bedroom.

As so often happens in our courts, judge and counsel set themselves up as arbiters of morals as well as of law. Davis had not been charged with any offence; he was a prosecution witness. Yet at both trials he was made to do public penance for writing the letters, being invited by Mr Dickens to say he was heartily ashamed of so doing. He complied. He was then asked just five questions by the prosecution, whose witness he was, and 50 by the defence. Mr Wild's cross-examination sought to persuade the jury that Davis was more intimate with Rose Harsent than he was prepared to admit.

Even though his testimony did not forge a link in the chain of circumstantial evidence the prosecution was trying to throw around Gardiner, Frederick Davis was able to shed light on a subject of historical interest - how sexual knowledge was obtained by young adults in a society that failed to provide any sex education in the home, the school or the church.

At the time of Rose Harsent's death Davis was living with his family in the house that adjoined Providence House. He was working as a junior assistant at Emmetts, the Peasenhall grocers and drapers, and two or three times a week he called at the back door of Providence House for orders. He denied ever having had sexual intercourse with Rose although they became very friendly. Their conversation touched on sexual matters, for Rose asked him to write down the bawdy limericks and verses bandied about by the lads of the village. This he did, and they formed the main part of the 'indecent missives'. They were probably far less obscene than those, for example, that today are printed in the Fleet Air Arm Song Book. If Rose had not enjoyed reading the letters she would have destroyed the first and refused to accept any more. Instead she kept them in her bedroom. Davis was asked to name the village lads who provided him with the verses - an utterly irrelevant question. He sidestepped by saying that all the lads in Peasenhall knew the verses.

These bawdy letters were not read out in court and so do not appear in the published transcripts of the trial. Copies were handed to the jury for their perusal. Only one letter written by Davis was made public; the one he said he wrote in what he called a flirting spirit. It ran:

> *Rose, my innermost yearnings have made me write down on paper a few lines about her who has enraptured my whole heart, a Rose among many thorns that reside in our midst. Her shapely form and wavy hair makes her the very ideal that I worship. She means to me my very existence. You*

may smile, fair reader, at my nonsense, but since she crossed my path the very moments spent in her company are like a breath from paradise. The time may come when she may leave me to woo some other man, but Heaven only knows the pain that will gnaw at my heart. Life will not be worth living; but should I win her heart for my very own it would seem like Heaven on earth. A glimpse of her at any time can cheer me through the day.... With her loving charms she has won my very soul, and when at night I sleepless lie, I think I see her face smiling at me as only those in love can know. I dare not think of her as being out of my reach; she has engraved her image upon my heart, and I pray that she will soon return my love. If not, Heaven only knows the consequences.

Burn this.

There are clear indications in this letter that Davis had copied many phrases from books he had read; he was by no means just a simple village lad. This was borne out by the fact that in September 1902 he had left Peasenhall to better himself in London but had to return for the first trial of Gardiner. At the time of the second trial he was unemployed. On the night of the thunderstorm he had gone to bed at half-past ten. He shared a bedroom with his brother and in order to go downstairs it was necessary to pass through the bedroom occupied by his parents.

Davis admitted that he had also given Rose a medical book; she had heard that another lad in the village possessed a copy and she was anxious to read it. The book was said to contain information on how to obtain an abortion, and with a show of moral indignation Mr Wild called it 'a dirty book'. Davis, annoyed by this description, said that in addition to information on abortion the book contained some useful recipes on how to cure chilblains and sweaty feet. He also admitted giving Rose a pamphlet entitled 'Proper Discipline to be Observed by Married People (birth control)'.

If the expert medical evidence about the time of Rose Harsent's death had not been particularly helpful to the jury because of its vagueness, that of another expert witness produced confusion by its complexity. The Crown called Thomas Henry Gurrin, a self-styled expert in handwriting who carried on business at 58 Holborn Viaduct, London, and he plunged into a description of vertical writing, similarities between various letters and words, the effect of different pen nibs and inks and other matters of interest to graphologists, using as specimens the letter of assignment, the envelope containing it, two letters written by Gardiner to his firm when he was at the Paris Exhibition, and a letter written to his wife while in custody. To complicate matters still further yet another letter was introduced for examination - an anonymous epistle confessing to the murder that had been sent to the ***East Anglian Daily Times***. The jury were supplied with photographs of these letters to help them follow the complex reasoning of the witness, who finally gave it as his opinion that Gardiner had written the letter of assignment.

Later the defence attempted to refute this opinion by producing its own expert witnesses on handwriting - James Fairbank, a chartered accountant and secretary of the Norfolk and Norwich Savings Bank, and Herbert Frederick Bayliss, chief clerk of the Holborn branch of the London and County Bank. It was part of Fairbank's job to examine handwriting and to detect forgeries. Bayliss's work entailed comparison of signatures. Both considered that Gardiner had not written the letter of assignment. In his summing up to the jury the judge seemed inclined to give more weight to the opinion of these two gentlemen than to Mr Gurrin.

According to the Yoxford postman, Frederick Henry Brewer, the letter of assignment had been posted at Peasenhall between half-past six on the Friday night and 10.55 the next morning, Saturday, May 31st, 1902. He delivered it to Providence House just after three o'clock on that Saturday afternoon. So it seemed the letter writer lived in or near Peasenhall, or had managed to get the letter posted there in order to make it appear that he lived in the village.

CHAPTER 7

The case for the defence was outlined by Mr Wild on the third day of the trial, Friday, January 23rd 1903, and afterwards he proceeded to call his witnesses. First he wanted to bring home to the jury that the murderer of Rose Harsent must have had bloodstained clothing - so Gardiner could not have killed her because no blood whatsoever was found on any of his clothing. Accordingly Dr William Alfred Elliston, J.P. of Stoke Hall, Ipswich and Villa Sandra, Felixstowe, was asked to give his expert opinion about the amount of blood likely to be caused by the throat wounds of the murdered woman.

Dr Elliston said that the cuts must have occasioned not only spurting but flowing of blood. The murderer could hardly have got away without some evidence of his guilt. The witness was not cross-examined by the Crown on this evidence.

Although at the Assizes it was customary to call the prisoner as the first major witness for the defence, Gardiner's counsel decided that the prisoner's wife should give her evidence before that of her husband. The ***East Anglian Daily Times*** noted that Mrs Georgina Gardiner wore a black hat most elaborately trimmed, and that she was looking much paler than on her appearance at the first trial.

Mrs Gardiner briefly recounted details of her family situation; she married Gardiner in October 1888, they had had eight children of whom six were alive - the eldest being 13 years of age, their married life had been happy, her spouse had been a good husband and father. In May 1901 she was made aware of the scandal circulating in the village about the alleged incident at the Doctor's Chapel. She was in bed at the time, just having been confined. The gossip made no difference to her relationship with her husband as she was convinced of his innocence. In addition she was on friendly terms with Rose Harsent who often called at the Gardiner home - and continued to do so even after the scandal had been spread abroad. She then spoke about the events of the 31st May, 1902, details of which have been given already, and of the lighting of the fire in the wash house on which they boiled a kettle for Sunday morning tea. Her husband took the children to Sunday school at half-past nine.

She did not hear of Rose Harsent's death until later in the morning after speaking to her next-door neighbour, Mrs Dickenson, who was on her way to church. A young man came past and told them that Rose Harsent had committed suicide. She recounted, too, the various visits the police had paid to the house and the clothes they had taken away. She had been shown the letter of assignation by Superintendent Staunton and he asked her if her husband wrote it. She told the police officer that it was not her husband's handwriting.

Just before the Court rose for lunch Mrs Gardiner had a violent fit of hysterics and had to be taken out of the room. She was not in a fit state to resume her evidence after lunch, so the prisoner went into the witness box. He was examined by Mr Wild and cross-examined by Mr Dickens.

According to Gardiner on the night of the incident at the Doctor's Chapel he had been to look at the horse in the stables at the Peasenhall works, for he was responsible for the animal, being in authority over the firm's horseman at that time. Outside the works he saw Rose Harsent by the gate to the pathway to the Chapel and she called to him and asked him to close the door of the Chapel as it had stuck. He did so, and after a brief conversation about hymns for the forthcoming Primitive Methodist anniversary they parted.

As for the statements of Henry Rouse concerning an alleged meeting between Rouse and Gardiner and Rose Harsent, the prisoner said this was a downright lie, as was Rouse's other allegation about Gardiner putting his legs on Rose's lap in chapel. The anonymous letter he had received did not mention this chapel incident and Gardiner said he did not know who had sent the letter until Rouse gave evidence at the first trial. But he could not suggest any motive for Rouse to act in that way, nor could he suggest a motive for Herbert Stammers to tell a lie about the time the wash-house fire was lit on the Sunday morning after Rose Harsent's murder.

He denied that he had written the letter making an appointment to see Rose at midnight on Saturday, May 21st, 1902.

Gardiner agreed he had been standing in the doorway of his house at about ten o'clock on the evening of the thunderstorm and that he went a few yards into the road to speak to Harry Burgess. Until he heard the evidence at the first trial he was unaware that the window of Rose Harsent's bedroom could be seen from the roadway outside his house. (Today the growth of trees prevents the window from being seen)

About a month or six weeks before the murder he had hulked a rabbit which had been bought from someone who brought it to the door, but he could not remember cleaning the knife afterwards.

The Old Chapel, Peasenhall. (now a youth club)

A number of other witnesses then gave short testimony for the defence. We have already dealt with that of the two business men, Fairbank and Bayliss, who were experienced in judging handwriting, and of Gardiner's solicitor, Leighton, who with friends had conducted an experiment at the Doctor's Chapel. Of the others, two whose testimony was helpful to Gardiner were Mrs Martha Walker of Sibton, and James Hart, a fowl and egg dealer of Ubbeston Green.

Mrs Walker was the local midwife and she had attended Mrs Gardiner at six confinements. She knew Rose Harsent and remembered an occasion in March 1902 when the two met at a tea meeting. Rose was suffering from a bad cold, and she told Mrs Walker that she had had some camphorated oil given to her by Mrs Gardiner. This confirmed the defence story that the broken bottle containing paraffin found in the kitchen of Providence House was the one Rose Harsent had taken away from the Gardiner home earlier in the year. Mrs Walker was also able to discredit the evidence of Henry Rouse in regard to the 'legs in the lap' story, for Mrs Walker attended the Sibton chapel and her daughter was a member of the choir. If Gardiner had put his legs on Rose's lap nearly all the people in the chapel would have seen it.

James Hart had slept at Peasenhall on the night of the thunderstorm and at four o'clock the following morning he began walking back to Ubbeston Green. He did not notice any footprints at the Peasenhall crossways or at the side of Providence House. He himself was wearing heavy hobnail boots. The implication was that Morriss ought to have seen Hart's footprints as well as those of the Indiarubber shoes, if footprints were indeed visible after a night of heavy rain.

On the morning of the fourth day of the trial Mrs Gardiner was brought in a cab from her lodgings in Ipswich where she had been staying, and she resumed her evidence . According to the **East Anglian Daily Times** her voice faltered at the outset and she seemed in danger of 'going off'; then she plucked up courage and answered every question with the utmost readiness and considerable spirit. She confirmed that Rose Harsent was a regular visitor to the Gardiner home, and that she (Mrs Gardiner) had never seen Rose guilty of impropriety with any man. She was emphatic that her husband had never walked out with Rose. As for Mr Rouse, Mrs Gardiner believed that he was jealous of her husband's position in the chapel, and that was the motive behind his testimony.

The trial was drawing to its close. Some obvious opportunities to clarify evidence had been missed. Neither prosecution nor defence asked Herbert Stammers if there was a smell of burning clothing coming from the Gardiners' washhouse. It was left to a juryman during the judge's summing up to put this question and the judge could give him no satisfaction. If clothes had been burnt early that Sunday morning all Gardiner's neighbours would have had the fumes blowing into their houses. But no witnesses were called to substantiate the testimony of Stammers.

The Wright and Skinner evidence, so crucial in proving an illicit relationship between Gardiner and Rose, was left unresolved; the prosecution relying on Constable Nunn's experiment that showed he could hear Wright and Skinner talking inside the Chapel, and Mr Leighton and friends testifying that no words spoken inside could be heard outside. The obvious course was for members of the jury to be taken to the Chapel to judge for themselves whether Wright and Skinner were telling the truth. Nobody suggested it.

There had been the customary abuse of witnesses and others by judge and counsel. At the first trial Mr Justice Grantham called Frederick Davis a disgrace to humanity. At the second trial Wright and Skinner, two young men who worked long hours at the factory, were called 'louts' by Mr Wild. Mr Justice Lawrance rudely shouted: 'Sit down. Be quiet' to Mr Crisp when he asked if he could be heard. No-one had the courtesy to explain to Mr Crisp why he was out of order. His omission from the list of prosecution witnesses remains a mystery, and is typical of the inefficiency that characterised the amassing of evidence against Gardiner.

Chapter 8

Mr. Ernest E. Wild made his closing speech for the defence and he was followed by Mr H.F.Dickens, K.C. making the final speech for the prosecution. What Mr Wild said was in essence a rebuttal of what Mr Dickens said after him, so it would be simpler if the main points of the prosecution's case were given with the defence's reply in brackets. The Crown suggested that ten points had to be complied with for the murderer to be identified and Mr Dickens was emphatic that Gardiner met all these requirements. He must have written like Gardiner (defence said that Gardiner did not write the letter of assignation; experts contradicted one another). He must have worn india-rubber shoes with a distinctive tread (defence said Gardiner had never worn india-rubber shoes found at his home. His brother in law had given them to Mrs Gardiner who had put them away in a cupboard.) He must have walked to and from Providence House that night (defence said that Gardiner's movements could be accounted for by witnesses, and that the alleged footprints never existed). He must have had a knife capable of inflicting the neck wounds (most working men carried knives; Gardiner used his for, among other things, 'hulking' rabbits). He must have had some connection with the broken medicine bottle (defence said that Rose was given it by Mrs Gardiner when she had a cold, and that Gardiner had never had it in his possession). He must have used buff envelopes in which the letter of assignment was sent (the type of buff envelope could be bought anywhere, and anyone at the Drill Works could have taken one from the work's office). He must have been able to see the light in Rose Harsent's bedroom (many people were about in Peasenhall that night; it was not only Gardiner who had the opportunity). He must have been looking for the light at 10 o'clock that night (again, many people were walking home or standing in their doorways at 10 o'clock). He must be a man in such a position it was imperative upon him to conceal his shame, - being responsible for Rose's pregnancy (the unknown man, whom the defence implied was responsible, was no doubt anxious to keep his good name but Gardiner had never formed an immoral association with Rose.)

Mr Justice Lawrance summed up, and at five o'clock on the afternoon of Saturday, 24th January 1903 the jury retired to consider its verdict. It returned to the court room at 7.12 pm. The foreman announced they had failed to agree on a verdict, and he was certain there was no chance of them agreeing. So the jury was discharged and Gardiner went back to prison presumably to await yet another trial. To order such a trial was left to the discretion of the Director of Public Prosecutions. Five days later he sent a telegram to Gardiner's solicitor stating that the prisoner would not be put on trial again. The governor of Ipswich Prison received an order to release Gardiner.

At the first trial the jury had voted eleven for and one against conviction. At the second trial on the same evidence the figures were exactly reversed, one for conviction and eleven against.

CHAPTER 9

The material given to Mr Dickens to secure a conviction was far from satisfactory. Is it not surprising that in a village of 700 inhabitants only three were to be found who said they had seen Gardiner and Rose Harsent in questionable circumstances? And two of these three - Wright and Skinner - were linked to the same incident. Is it possible for a married man and a servant girl in a small community to have an affair lasting more than a year without it being noticed by a number of people - especially after the village had been alerted by scandalous gossip started by Wright and Skinner. Did this failure to find witnesses mean there had never been an affair between the two?

If the police file on the case is still in existence it might throw light on how the investigation was conducted. Was there an house-to-house enquiry to find villagers who might have seen Gardiner and Rose together? Why was no thorough search made of the Gardiner home, instead of the piecemeal requests for items of clothing? A search of the premises, even three or for days after Gardiner had been arrested, might have revealed in the ashes of the wash-house traces of clothing having been burnt, if Gardiner had indeed done such a thing.

As it was the prosecution had to make do with a team of witnesses none of whom carried total conviction. The medical experts could give no clear indication of the time of Rose Harsent's death, thus making it more difficult for the prosecution to focus on a particular time in Gardiner's account of his movements on the night of May 31st June 1st. The handwriting expert's arguments were so complex, and so many examples from five documents were given, that they confused the jury. And since Mr Gurrin's conclusions had been refuted by handwriting experts called by the defence it could well be that the jury agreed with the judge who said in his summing up: 'I do not place the greatest reliance upon expert evidence.'

The other major witnesses for the prosecution all had a question mark hanging over them. Why was it that James Morriss and Herbert

Stammers had not gone to the police with their evidence when news of Gardiner's arrest became known? Why did Henry Rouse tell the story of Gardiner putting his feet on Rose Harsent's lap during a chapel service? Why did he get his wife to write an anonymous letter to Gardiner and then not mention the feet-on-the-lap incident that sparked off the letter? Did the police try to find any member of the congregation who saw that alleged happening? In the event it was the defence who produced a chapel member to say it could not possibly have happened without nearly all the congregation seeing it. The whole of Rouse's testimony became suspect in consequence. Perhaps Mrs Gardiner was correct when she said Rouse was jealous of her husband. Gardiner had been entrusted with a number of official positions in the chapel; Rouse had come down in the world, having once been a farmer, then a bailiff and, at the time of the trial, a roadman.

And what of Wright and Skinner? Mr Dickens asked the jury in his closing speech: 'Why should these witnesses be guilty of telling the most diabolical lies without having the slightest motive for lying?' One possible answer is that the two young men had no idea, at the time of the Chapel incident, that they would ever be called to give evidence at the Assizes. This is how it might have happened.

Like many working-class villagers they led narrow and restricted lives. For the most part their leisure was spent in and around the village

The Drill Works and Stable.

for they had no means of going farther afield. Not surprisingly they were always on the look-out for entertainment. Wright saw Gardiner go along the path to the Chapel where Rose Harsent had already gone. Straightway he went down into Peasenhall Street and brought Skinner from his lodgings so that they could go back to the Chapel together to see what was going on. Gardiner, as he said in his evidence, had managed to close the Chapel door which was stuck, and he and Rose had departed. If this was true then Wright and Skinner would arrive to find no-one there. So Wright went away, leaving Skinner alone outside the Chapel, and when Wright returned twenty minutes later Skinner 'had him on', saying he had heard two people inside the Chapel talking, and he retailed his story of the 38th chapter of Genesis. Almost certainly Skinner wouid have known this chapter for the Bible has always been a valuable source of knowledge on sexual behaviour for children who have to pick up 'the facts of life' where they can. Skinner might even haye been a choirboy in his earlier days- they are experts on the 'best' bits of the Bible as they have time, during the boring sermons, to look them up.

Skinner enjoys making up this story and soon he and Wright are laughing and joking about it. Wright knows by now of course, that there is no-one in the Chapel and that Skinner has concocted the story for a bit of fun. They go down the road into Peasenhall and mect another youth. They 'have him on' by telling him the story as if it were true. The friend goes away, believing the story, and tells other people. Wright and Skinner have had their little joke and think no more about it. But the damage has been done. People approach them during the next few days and ask them: Is it true? Suddenly the two young men have gained in esteem; other folk are seeking them out, asking for the juicy anecdote to be recounted yet again. For once in their lives Wright and Skinner have some status in the village. Rather than forego this, and to avoid losing face and being called liars, they stick to the story.

There is now no turning back. When Gardiner asks them to apologise they refuse, knowinq the weakness of his case, for it is only his word and that of Rose Harsent's against theirs. The Sibton Chapel enquiry supports this view; the result was deadlock. So they are not greatly perturbed when Gardiner threatens legal action; if he couldn't get the decision at the enquiry at his own chapel he will not be successful at law. And when Gardiner does not take legal action, after threatening to do so in a solicitor's letter, they feel even more secure. Finally, a year later, they are approached by the police, and their fabricated story becomes crucial evidence at a murder trial. They are now very important people, having time off from work to make statements to the police, being given transport to the Magistrates Court and to the Ipswich Assizes. Their little joke has snowballed into a life and death matter for William Gardiner. If they had recanted at the Assizes what would have happened to them? One can imagine the judge uttering scathing remarks about 'young liars'. They would be in bad odour with the police, outcasts in the village, and faced with the possibility of prosecution for wasting police time or perhaps perjury. So they stuck to their story, consoling themselves with the thought that it was not only their evidence that might send Gardiner to the gallows; they were just two of many witnesses.

I have dealt with this aspect of the case at some length because the desire to shine, to be someone of importance, is dear to the heart of many people especially those who for a number of reasons (education, inherited characteristics, home life) are not likely to make their mark in life. The evidence of James Morriss, the assistant gamekeeper, can be looked at in the same light. He might have seen one or two footprints near Gardiner's house; it is extremely unlikely after a night of rain he would have seen a double set stretching 208 yards and clearly visible both outside Gardiner's house and Providence House. But Morriss knows the Gardiner/Rose Harsent anecdote and he gets a little bit of status by embroidering the story and telling it to the head gamekeeper. It was a startling coincidence that Rose Harsent's dead body should have been discovered a few hours after Morriss had made up this story. He was a little alarmed when the implications of his falsehood became clear to him, so he avoided going to the police. However, as with Wright and Skinner, the damage had been done. The head gamekeeper told someone else, the police were told, Morriss was interviewed. Was he then to lose face with the head gamekeeper (making him look a liar), was he also to forego the experience of being someone of importance in the village? He stuck to his story.

'Why should Stammers be guilty of the grossest perjury?' asked Mr Dickens in his closing speech for the prosecution. 'People do not act without motives; they are not so recklessly wicked as to send a man to his doom without some feeling against him of hostility or ill-will.' The implication here is that Herbert Stammers who testified about the wash-house fire would have no ill-will or hostility towards the prisoner. Gardiner himself said that he had never had a quarrel with Stammers and could not suggest why his neighbour should have invented the story of the wash-house fire being alight at 7.30 am. But the two men were not on friendly terms. Although they had been neighbours for three or four years they only passed the time of day. We do not know what feelings Stammers had about Gardiner; he could have been harbouring resentment against him for some rift between the families that happened a long time ago which had never been forgotten by Stammers.

In life people bear grudges for many years, never revealing them to anyone. But given the opportunity a decision can be taken, a vote cast, to work off some of the bitterness, to give an outlet for emotions never outwardly expressed. It is just barristers' blarney to suggest as Mr Dickens did that there was no reason for Stammers to perjure himself. We do not know what his feelings were towards Gardiner. On another occasion, at another trial, we might well have heard Mr Dickens declaim: 'Who can plumb the depths of the human soul?'

Alternatively it might have been a desire by Stammers to be important. Villagers would look to him for some tit-bit of information as he lived next door to Gardiner. So he invented the tale of the wash-house fire being lit earlier than usual on the morning of the murder. Is it not strange that Stammers did not take this important piece of information to the police? Instead, the police heard it second-hand and then went to see him.

Because the Peasenhall murder was never

resolved the story presents crime writers with a beanfeast. For nearly every piece of evidence two or more explanations can be found. And if we wish to speculate on the identity of the 'unknown man' whom the defence claimed committed the murder then there are several characters in the drama, now dead,who can have the mantle of murderer draped around them by fiction writers. Consider the suggestion that it might have been William Crisp, Rose Harsent's employer. Rose was never seen going about with a man (apart from the Gardiner allegations), but she had every opportunity inside Providence House of becoming intimate with her employer. We know nothing of Mr Crisp except that his wife said he did not want to go downstairs to investigate the scream. We know very little about Mrs Crisp either; in the fictional story she might be shielding her husband or actively assisting him. Why was he never called to give evidence? An objection to this theory springs to mind; Crisp would not have written a letter of assignment, for Rose was already under his roof. The objection can be overruled by suggesting that the man who wrote the letter was Rose's lover (or one of them) and that he had no intention of murdering her. There may have been one or two men in the kitchen of Providence House that night, not necessarily at the same time.

A second plot might be woven around the man to whom Rose was engaged to be married in 1900. We do not know who he was or why the engagement was broken. Suppose he felt hostility towards her, or - at the other end of the scale - was still seeing her and having intercourse with her.

The copy of ***The Trial of William Gardiner*** in my possession once belonged to Mrs Erskine Muir of Southwold, a student of criminology who gave lectures on famous criminal cases. In a note in the book she writes: 'Alderman Jenkins of Southwold, who was then a young photographer, was employed by the police to take photographs. He told me in 1952 that actually from evidence in the kitchen there was no doubt that a man had been there, and that Rose and the man had intercourse that night.'

No mention was made of this at the trial, but it does increase the possibility that there were two visitors to the kitchen of Providence House on the night Rose Harsent was murdered. One went to make love to Rose. The other went to kill her because he had a reputation to guard and she had threatened to expose him as the father of her unborn child.

Although both defence and prosecution counsels agreed that Frederick William Davis, the writer of the 'indecent missives' to Rose, was not concerned in the murder their reasons seem perfunctory. Davis stated in the witness box that he could not have got out of the house without his parents knowing, because - owing to the design of the house - he would have to pass through his parents' bedroom and they would wake up. But suppose his parents had been to The Swan that night and slept heavily as a result... And was it not possible for Davis to climb through his own bedroom window into the garden below, and then go through the fence into the back yard of Providence House? Research has revealed another interesting item concerning Davis. According to the Police Register for 1902 (which is still in existence) Davis with another youth had appeared a few months earlier before the Saxmundham magistrates charged with an assault on a girl. The case against them was dismissed.

Peasenhall Parish Church.

Yet another character whom the crime writer could turn into the murderer was Dr Lay. There was no need for Rose and the local doctor to be seen together; their friendship could ripen in the doctor's surgery. And consider the unusual behaviour of Dr Lay at the scene of the crime. Although Constable Nunn was in charge of proceedings until his superior arrived, Dr Lay picked up the label on the medicine bottle and put it in his pocket 'for safe keeping'. Was it the same label that was later handed to Superintendent Staunton? A freshly-written label, suitably treated with paraffin and blood, could have been substituted in order to implicate William Gardiner who was already under suspicion because of the Wright and Skinner gossip.

Even James Morriss could be regarded as a suspect. If he had killed Rose Harsent that night he might have had the idea of pointing the evidence away from him and towards someone else. Who better than William Gardiner about whom there had already been a scandal linking his name with Rose Harsent's? A fanciful crime writer might have had Morriss putting on a pair of india-rubber shoes and making the footprints himself, hoping that some would still be visible later in the day to verify his story.

These are just some of the possibilities that the Peasenhall murder presents to the writer of fiction. They should be read as that - fiction - and not taken as libellous comment on people long since dead who are not able to defend their reputation.

CHAPTER 10

When Gardiner received the news of his release he fell on his knees and thanked God for his deliverance. After shaving off his moustache and beard he caught the night train from Ipswich to London.

We do not know what passed between him and his wife in the interim between the end of the trial and the release. Possibly they agreed it would be better, if Gardiner gained his freedom, for them to move away from Peasenhall and start family life again elsewhere. It would have been extremely uncomfortable for Gardiner had he returned to the village for many of the inhabitants believed in his guilt. His wife would have been tolerated because there was a great deal of sympathy for her, and admiration for the way she had faced the ordeal of two trials, but the children would have been given a rough time by their schoolmates. So, as soon as it could be arranged, Mrs Gardiner and the children left Peasenhall. The gossip that has been handed down to the present generation of villagers is that Gardiner and his wife did not resume married life together, but this may be incorrect. At first Gardiner obtained work as a grocer's assistant in South London, and his family may have joined him there.

Before his marriage he had been friendly with a Wangford girl, Miss Bella Newberry, and there is reliable evidence that some time after the trial she received a letter from him. By then she was a-happily married woman. My informant (a relative of Miss Newberry) remembers that the letter came from North America, but cannot say for certain whether it was Canada or the United States. So it seems likely the Gardiner family may have emigrated.

During 1981 two matters came to light of interest in the case. The Police Register for 1902 was discovered; this shows that when Gardiner was first charged by the police he gave his age as 35. Yet Mr Dickens in his opening speech refers to Gardiner as being 'something like forty-five years of age'. What are we to believe?

Secondly Mrs Michael Lambton and her son, who were staying at the Ancient House, Peasenhall, on holiday, conducted an experiment at the Doctor's Chapel (that today is within the grounds of the Ancient House). They found that words spoken in normal conversation inside the Chapel could be heard clearly by any-one standing outside. So Wright and Skinner may have been telling the truth, and William Gardiner and Rose Harsent might have been having an affair. But this does not prove that Gardiner was the murderer.

The question remains unanswered: who killed Rose Harsent?